I Wanna Iguana

KAREN KAUFMAN ORLOFF • ILLUSTRATED BY DAVID CATROW

G. P. PUTNAM'S SONS • NEW YORK

G. P. Putnam's Sons, a division of Penguin Young Readers Group, 345 Hudson Street, New York, NY 10014. G. P. Putnam's Sons,
Reg. U.S. Pat. & Tm. Off.
Published simultaneously in Canada. Manufactured in China by South China Printing Co. Ltd.
Designed by Marikka Tamura. Text set in Catchup and Comic Sans. The art was done in pencil and watercolor.
Library of Congress Cataloging-in-Publication Data
Orloff, Karen Kaufman. I wanna iguana / Karen Kaufman Orloff ; illustrated by David Catrow. p. cm.
Summary: Alex and his mother write notes back and forth in which Alex tries to persuade her to let him have a baby iguana for a pet.
[1. Iguanas as pets—Fiction. 2. Pets—Fiction. 3. Letters—Fiction. 4. Mothers and sons—Fiction.] I. Catrow, David, ill.
II. Title. PZ7.O6332Iw 2004 [E]—dc21 2002010895
ISBN 0-399-23717-8
5 7 9 10 8 6 4

To Max and Emily
for their inspiration,
to Brad for his support,
and to all my writer friends
for making me work harder. —K.K.O.

*To Mr. Alexander—
you taught me discipline
and how to be an artist. —D.C.*

Dear Mom,
I know you don't think I should have Mikey Gulligan's baby iguana when he moves, but here's why I should. If I don't take it, he goes to Stinky and Stinky's dog, Lurch, will eat it. You don't want that to happen, do you?

Signed,
Your sensitive son,
Alex

Dear Alex,

I'm glad you're so compassionate,
but I doubt that Stinky's mother
will let Lurch get into
the iguana's cage.
Nice try, though.

Love,
Mom

SEE!?

Dear Mom,

Did you know that iguanas are really quiet and they're cute too. I think they are much cuter than hamsters.

Love,
Your adorable son,
Alex

Dear Alex,

Tarantulas are quiet too, but I wouldn't want one as a pet. By the way, that iguana of Mikey's is uglier than Godzilla. Just thought I'd mention it.

Love,
Mom

Dear Mom,

You would never even have to see the iguana. I'll keep his cage in my room on the dresser next to my soccer trophies. Plus, he's so small, I bet you'll never even know he's there.

Love and a zillion and one kisses,

Alex

Dear Alex,

Iguanas can grow to be over six feet long. You won't have enough space in your whole room, much less on your dresser (with or without your trophies).

Love,

Mom

Dear Mom,

It takes 15 years for an iguana to get that big. Mikey told me. I'll be married by then and probably living in my own house.

Love,

Your smart and mature kid, Alex

Dear Alex,

How are you going to get a girl to marry you when you own a six-foot-long reptile?

Love,

Your concerned mother

Dear Mom,
Forget the girl.
I need a new friend now!

This iguana can be the brother I've always wanted.
Love,
Your lonely child, Alex

Dear Alex,
You have a brother.
Love,
Mom

Dear Mom,
I know I have a brother but he's just a baby. What fun is that? If I had an iguana, I could teach it tricks and things. Ethan doesn't do tricks. He just burps and poops.
Love,
Grossed-out Alex

Dear Alex,

How do I know you're ready for a pet? Remember what happened when you took home the class fish?

Love,

Mom

Dear Mom,

If I knew the fish was going to
jump into the spaghetti sauce,
I never would have taken
the cover off the jar!

Love,
Your son who has
learned his lesson

P.S. Iguanas don't like spaghetti.

Dear Alex,
Let's say I let you have
the iguana on a trial basis.
What exactly would you do
to take care of it?
Love,
Mom

Dear Mom,
I would feed him every day (he eats lettuce). And I would make sure he had enough water. And I would clean his cage when it got messy.
Love,
Responsible Alex
P.S. What's a trial basis?

Dear Alex,

A trial basis means Dad and I see how well you take care of him for a week or two before we decide if you can have him forever. Remember, Stinky and Lurch are waiting!

Love,

Mom

P.S. If you clean his cage as well as you clean your room, you're in trouble.

Dear Mom,

I'll really, really, really try to clean my room and the iguana's cage. Also, listen to this. I'll pay for the lettuce with my allowance. I mean, how much can one baby iguana eat, anyway?

Love,

Alex the financial wizard

"Are you sure you want to do this, Alex?"

"Yes, Mom!
I wanna iguana....
Please!"

Dear Alex,
Look on your dresser.
Love,
Mom

"YESSSS!
Thank you!
Thank
you!"